The Fi

I was sitting in my office staring at the frosted glass of the door. It was a cold and rainy October morning and I had a hangover that made my head feel as faded and peeled as the paint on the walls. A sharp rapping came that I thought at first was my brain shattering. Looking through the frosted glass I could see the form of the rapper. It was a woman, and a good looker by the shadow.

The door opened and she stepped into the darkened office. Her eyes a soft green-gray would have been level with my own if I had been standing. Remembering my manners a moment later I was. She smiled at my courtesy and her warm, red lips almost made my legs melt beneath me.

"I wish to employ your services, Mr. Slade. A friend of mine died recently under mysterious circumstances. The police are saying that it was either an accident or suicide. I have reason to believe it was murder."

With those words, private eye Frank Slade embarks on the strangest case of his career, one that will threaten his very existence.

The Fictional Detective

A Fictional Press Novel by

Greg Fowlkes

The Fictional Detective

© 2009 Greg Fowlkes

All rights reserved. No part of this book may be used or reproduced in any manner without written permission except for brief quotations for review purposes.

Published by Intrepid Ink, LLC

Intrepid Ink, LLC provides full publishing services to authors of fiction and non-fiction books, eBooks and websites. From editing to formatting, to publishing, to marketing, Intrepid Ink gets your creative works into the hands of the people who want to read them.

Find out more at www.IntrepidInk.com.

ISBN 10:   0984385703
ISBN 13:   9780984385706

Printed in the United States of America

The Fictional Detective

Chapter 1

I was sitting in my office staring at the frosted glass of the door. It was a cold and rainy Friday morning in October and I had a hangover that made my head feel as faded and peeled as the paint on the walls. The half empty glass of Jack Daniel's wasn't helping my head any, but it was making it easier to ignore some of my other problems. Like how I was going to pay three months back rent on the eight by ten closet the landlord chose to call an office. Jobs had been pretty scarce lately. Even the divorce business had fallen off. No one seemed to care what their spouse was up to anymore. Not for the first time I wondered what the world was coming to.

A sharp rapping sound came that I thought at first

was my brain shattering. A second later I realized that it was the tap of knuckles on the glass of the door. The lights were off in the office, and it couldn't have looked very promising from the outside, but the knuckles kept up the rapping. Looking through the "evitceteD ,EDALS KNARF", printed backwards on the frosted glass I could see the form of the rapper silhouetted by the sixty watt bulb in the hallway. It was a woman, and a good looker by the shadow.

The rapping stopped and the shadow moved away. I cursed myself for being too slow, but then she returned and rapped once more. The knuckles had a sort of desperate sound to them so I told her to come in, trying to keep my voice from sounding too harsh. The door opened hesitantly and she stepped through into the darkened office. She stood in the doorway groping for the light switch.

The bank of overhead fluorescents came on with a stutter and the light made me wince. I didn't mind so much when I got a good look at the dame. Her shadow hadn't done her justice at all. She was tall, looking taller on her spiked heels. Her eyes, a soft green-gray would have almost been level with my own if I had been standing. Remembering my manners a moment later, I was. She smiled at my courtesy and her warm, red lips almost made my legs melt beneath me. Blonde hair curled under just at her shoulder line. I got a good look at it up close when I stepped forward to help her out of her coat; it looked natural. Everything about her looked natural though she was too good to believe.

I don't normally go overboard treating women with respect. These days it doesn't really pay, but this broad had class. Under her coat she was dressed in a black dress that clung to her like a sheath from her neck to her nylon clad calves, but despite the sensuous curves she looked like she was in mourning.

I held out a chair for her and then took one myself. Self-consciously I put the cap back on the bottle of whiskey and put it and the glass away in a drawer. "What can I do for you, Miss . . . ?" I couldn't see if she had a wedding ring on underneath her gloves, but I had the distinct impression that she wasn't married.

"Janet, Janet Nielsen," she said in a soft voice that reminded me of the taste of good bourbon -- smooth and mellow but with a bite to it. "You are Mr. Frank Slade, are you not?"

"That's what it says on the door," I answered. She hadn't made a mistake. I had no illusions about my reputation and Miss Nielsen looked like she had the money and the class to get the best in town.

"I wish to employ your services if you are available, Mr. Slade. It's a matter of some importance to me and I am quite willing to pay you well if you can start immediately."

"I think I can shift my schedule, Miss Nielsen," I said,

aware that I had no schedule or clients either. "What is it you want me to do? You didn't correct me when I said 'Miss', so I'm guessing you don't want me to check up on an errant husband. Or do you?"

"No, nothing like that," she said with a note of distaste. "A friend of mine died recently under mysterious circumstances. The police are saying that it was either an accident or suicide. I have reason to believe it was murder."

"Look, Miss Nielsen," I said, "I'd like to help you out, but if it's murder, it's a business for the cops and I can't get involved. I could lose my license."

"But if the police say that it's not murder, then you are free to investigate. That's right, isn't it?" she said, assuredly. I wasn't used to getting that much logic out of a woman. "I will pay you two hundred dollars a day plus expenses. That will be adequate, I believe. I have a thousand dollars here as an advance against the first five days."

She opened her purse and pulled out ten crisp, new hundred dollar bills and laid them out on the blotter of my desk. I needed that money, but I was getting a little suspicious of the whole thing. It was too much like the opening of a detective novel; a beautiful woman, a hard-boiled private investigator, a stack of brand new large denomination bills.

"Look, I'm still not sure I can do anything for you.

Why don't I take a day's pay and check things out with the cops? If I think I can do anything for you, I'll come back and get the rest of the money. If not, we can call it even." I looked into those gray-green eyes. She hesitated for a moment, and then nodded. I slid two bills from the pile, and then slid the rest back towards her. She didn't pick them up.

"Okay. Now why don't you tell me who this friend of yours was, and how he died?" I was watching her closely for her reaction as I asked.

"Do you know of Ezekial O. Handler?"

"The mystery writer?" I asked.

"Yes," she answered. For the first time she seemed to lose some of her composure. I wondered why. Handler was pretty well known as a writer. He had written a dozen or more books, a couple of which had made the best seller lists. I'd met him once or twice in the course of my work, but we definitely did not move in the same circles.

"Last night his car went off the road along West Shore Drive. They said it was traveling at a high rate of speed and crashed through the barrier. The car burned and Ezekial burned with it."

"That sounds like an ordinary traffic accident to me, Miss Nielsen," I said, trying not to sound callous.

"But it couldn't have been. He was a very good driver. He never took chances, either. Not stupid ones, at least. He wasn't the kind of man who felt that he had to prove anything, least of all to himself. No, if his car crashed there was a reason for it."

"If there was, I'm sure the police will find it," I said. I didn't like what I had to say next, she obviously had some sort of emotional tie to Handler, but in my business there are a lot of things you have to do that you don't like. "That is if it was an accident. It might have been a suicide. I didn't know Handler personally, but writers aren't always the most stable sort of people. It goes with the artistic temperament. Could he have had any reason for killing himself?"

"No, of course not," she said very defensively. "He had everything to live for. He was well off financially, he had a lot of good friends, he'd just finished his last book and it was one of his best. He stood to make a good deal of money from it, at least a million dollars. He was a happy man, Mr. Slade. I know that he was."

"Just what was your relationship to Handler, Miss Nielsen? Why are you so interested in proving that he was murdered?"

I thought she might clam up then or get huffy, but she said right out loud, "I was his mistress." Just like that, not like she was ashamed of it or anything.

Maybe she wasn't. These days who could tell? "I loved him, Mr. Slade, and if he was murdered I want the murderer brought to justice."

I raised my eyebrows at that. Handler had pushed past fifty as far as I knew and he wasn't much of a looker, either. The pictures on his book jackets showed a nose that had been broken in fights a couple of times. When I'd seen him he'd proved to be a short man, though powerfully built. He had a reputation for getting into fights. He didn't seem the sort that would appeal to the woman across the desk from me, but like I always said, who can tell these days.

"I know what you're thinking, that he was thirty years older than me, but I never cared about that. He was always very good to me, kind and gentle. I admit to being a kept woman, Mr. Slade, but that doesn't mean that I didn't love him."

There was something strange about that phrase - kept woman - that seemed out of place. It was more like something from one of Handler's books than what a young, liberated woman should be saying. I didn't doubt that it was true, though. It would explain where Nielsen's money came from. Listening to her, I could believe that she had loved him, too. Either that or she was a mighty good actress.

"I'll take your word for it that he was wealthy and

happy, but there are other reasons a man kills himself. What about his past? Could there be some secret there? Or his health? Hemingway killed himself because of cancer, after all." Handler wasn't quite in the same league, but I hoped the comparison might mollify her a little. The last couple of questions hadn't improved her opinion of me.

"I don't know too much about his past. He never talked much about it. He always seemed to live in the present. He's been a public figure for twenty-five years, though. I don't think he could have had many secrets. He never seemed to care what people thought about him anyway, as long as they read his books."

"Maybe he cared about what you thought?" I said.

She smiled at that and I thought I was going to melt again. "No, I don't think so. He was fond of me, but the love was all one way. The only opinions that really matters to him were his own. He never seemed to mind the critics."

"What about his health, then? He was getting on in years."

"I can assure you; he kept in very good shape. He always ran four or five miles before he'd start writing in the morning. He was in good shape other ways, too," she said in a wistful tone that made me wish I'd been the late Mr. Handler. "He'd just been to a doctor a couple of weeks ago for an insurance examination. They must not have found any problems because he got the policy." I could believe her on that. Handler had been something of a physical fitness nut. I could remember the deep chest and the boxer's shoulders.

"Well, we'll rule out suicide for the moment," I said. "But he still might have had an accident. Some drunken fool might have run him off the road. It could have happened. If so, I'm afraid you'll just have to face it. But I'll check with the cops and go out and look at the scene of the crash myself. If I see anything suspicious I'll check up on it, Miss Nielsen."

"Thank you, I'm sure you will. Will that be all, now?"

"Yes, I think so. If I have any more questions I'll get in touch with you." She gave me her address and phone number, then rose to leave.

"Miss Nielsen?"

"Yes?"

"You forgot your eight hundred dollars," I said, though part of me was cursing myself being for a fool.

"Thank you, Mr. Slade," she said, picking up the bills and dropping them into her purse. I helped her on with her coat, smelling again the warm, sweet scent of her hair.   Then she was gone.

Chapter 2

Her perfume lingered in the office after she left and it took me a few minutes to pull myself together. Then I decided it was time for me to earn my two hundred dollars for the day. Pulling on my trench coat I headed for the parking garage where I kept my car.

I didn't have many details on Handler's death so I stopped off at the corner newsstand on the way to the garage to pick up the morning paper. Handler had been somebody, and there was sure to be something in the paper about his death.

There was. When Armand passed a copy of the morning edition over the counter the story was splashed over the bottom half of the front page, "Mystery Writer Killed in Auto Crash." There was a picture underneath the headlines of a charred hulk resting on the rocks. It didn't look too pretty.

"Too bad about Meester Handler, ees eet not Meester Slade?" Armand asked. I nodded to him. Armand O'Hara had been a jockey once until a horse had fallen and crushed his right leg. Rather than go back to Puerto Rico he had bought the newsstand. I paid him a few dollars now and then for information. He heard a lot. Being short and Spanish speaking a lot of people tended to ignore him when they were having conversations, but that was their mistake.

"He was here just yesterday," Armand said sadly.

"Did he stop here often?" I asked off handedly. If Armand was volunteering information, I wasn't going to object.

"Yes, often. Hees publisher has an office just down the street. Hee stop here many times, buy newspaper, magazine. Funny thing, he always buy stuff about occult, magic, spiritos, that sort of thing. Hee didn't seem the kind of man who would be interested in such things. Very macho man, Meester Handler. Good with the chacitas."

"Yeah," I said ruefully thinking of Miss Nielsen. "I don't know, Armand. Maybe he was thinking of using that stuff in one of his books. You know, research."

"Yes, the mysteries," the newsboy nodded solemnly as if the explanation was important to him. "You must be right, Meester Slade. Meester Handler's books were always so real."

I gave him a buck for the paper and told him to keep the change, feeling just a little guilty for pumping him without paying. I read the paper on the way to the garage. There wasn't much to it, just some stuff about who he had been and about his books. There was some speculation about alcohol, but no proof. There hadn't been an autopsy yet. Not a word about suicide, but that didn't surprise me. Until there was official word from the coroner any such speculation might get the paper a law suit.

The stretch of West Shore Drive where Handler had gone off was a twisty bit of road. I took it about thirty five in my old Chevy convertible, glad that the rain had thinned out. It had been foggy the night before. Despite what Miss Nielsen had said it was easy to imagine somebody, even a good driver, cold sober, going off the road if he had tried to push it at all.

It wasn't hard to find the spot where the accident had occurred. The rail had been torn out for about forty feet. Also, there was a police wrecker and a squad car parked on the side of the road. When I had parked and looked over the rail, I could see that they were still in the process of hauling the car up off the rocks below. It was a nasty drop there. The embankment was a good fifty feet high, not shear, but plenty steep. There were rocks sticking up out of the lake. The car had piled into one of those and burst into flame when the gas tank ruptured. The stone was blackened and cracked from the heat.

One of the uniform cops was about to shoo me away

when I spotted Lt. Flannigan climbing around on the rocks down below. I called out to him and he waved to the cop that it was all right for me to hang around. I took that as an invitation and found the place that all the cops and lab boys had been using to get down to the wreck. It was a steep climb, but I made it by hanging onto the roots of some bushes sticking out of the hill face.

"What are you doin' around here, Slade? I thought peepin' through keyholes and transoms was more your trade?"

I didn't take the bait, knowing he was just trying to annoy me. "Just curious, Lieutenant. I wanted to know what could make you get out and get your shoes dirty."

Flannigan looked down at his brogans, then flushed and smiled. "Handler was a very famous person. Only the department's best for the late lamented author."

"You don't sound too sympathetic," I stated.

"No, the creep got drunk, drove his car too fast and didn't make the last curve. So everybody has to get up in the middle of the night and stand out in the rain until we can get the body. I should be sympathetic to that?"

"The coroner said he was drinking, then?" I asked.

"Not yet. Maybe never. The body was pretty badly burned up. There wasn't a whole lot left. He'd lain in the water for a while, too. The car ended up upside down, you see," he said, pointing at the hulk of the Jaguar E-Type. "He burned inside, then when the flames got to the seat belt he fell out of the car and into the water. The crash happened about eleven last night. We didn't get the call until about three. That's pretty strange when you think about it. The car must have gone up like a torch. You should have been able to see it for a mile even in last night's weather."

"It can be a lonely stretch of road late at night."

Flannigan shrugged noncommittally. "Well, it took us another two hours to get to the body. It had been burnt, immersed, and then bashed around by the rocks for a couple of hours. I don't think the coroner will be able to say much one way or another."

"They can do quite a bit with just a little," I said helpfully.

"You didn't see the body. They hauled it out of here in garbage bags. Three of them. Why the interest, Slade? Insurance? If so, they're going to have a hard time proving suicide."

"You think it might have been suicide?"

"It could be, but I doubt it. Be hell to prove it like I said. Bad weather, twisty road. I'm surprised we didn't have a couple of more accidents along here last night."

It was my turn to nod solemnly.

"Funny, though. There was an insurance man poking around here earlier before we got the body out. Handler had just taken out a policy on his life. Two hundred and fifty big ones. It pays double in case of accidental death. If he was thinking about offing himself he sure made arrangements to take care of someone."

"Did the insurance man say who the beneficiary was?" I asked, trying to sound merely curious. Technically it wasn't the sort of information I was supposed to have.

"It goes to some broad he'd been shackin' up with. A man his age," Flannigan said with disapproval.

"Her name wouldn't be Janet Nielsen, would it?"

"How'd you find that out, Slade? And you still haven't told me what you're doing here."

"Handler's mistress hired me to investigate his death. She said that she suspected foul play. Maybe she just wants to make sure the insurance company doesn't try to ice her out by calling it suicide," I suggested. I didn't figure it that way, but it was an excuse the lieutenant could understand and live with.

"Yeah, that's the sort of thing you'd expect from a bimbo that sleeps with a man twice her age. And Handler not even dead a day yet. What's this world coming to, Slade?"

"I keep asking myself the same question, Flannigan."

They were about ready to haul the car up to the road so I took the chance to look inside. There wasn't much to see, but Flannigan had been right. Handler had had his seatbelt fastened, both the lap belt and the shoulder harness. Not the sort of thing one expects from a suicide or a careless driver. The car had a lot of miles on it, but it was in good shape, or had been until the crash. It didn't quite smell right, though there was nothing that I could pin it on for sure.

"There isn't any chance that it was foul play, is there?"

"Naw, not that I can see. The lab boys say that the brakes hadn't been tampered with or anything like that. The only tire marks on the road up above are Handler's. Not even skid marks, just the impressions in the shoulder where he went off. Like I said, an accident."

"You don't mind if I keep looking into it then? I

could use the money," I said, truthfully.

"Sure, go ahead. As far as I'm concerned, it's a closed case. Just keep out of the way and don't go giving your suspicions to the press. The commissioner is going to be pretty sensitive about that. This thing will get enough publicity as it is."

They had started winching the car up the hillside. There wasn't much more to see, so I followed Flannigan back up to the road. "You ever read much of Handler's stuff?" I asked just to make conversation.

"You kidding? I never read that crap. I get enough murder and rape at work to have to read about it in books. That stuff is never real, anyway. Just a lot of crap."

"I don't know. I've heard that Handler's stuff was pretty realistic. That's why it sold so good."

"Have you read any of it?" Flannigan asked as he got into his car.

"Naw, I never read any of that crap," I said and left him with his jaw flapping.

I spent the rest of the afternoon trying to butter up some contacts that I had in the coroner's office. They were a little more clam mouthed than usual and it took me a fifty to get anywhere. When I finally read a Xerox of the autopsy report I wondered if it had been worth it.

The cause of death was listed as burning, complicated by multiple contusions and a broken leg. No surprises there. There had been no water in the lungs, Handler had been dead before he entered the water, but that just bore out what I had heard from Flannigan. There was a lot of medical double talk about the grizzly details, but it all added up to the fact that Handler had died in a flaming car crash that ended up in the lake. Traces of alcohol had been found in the blood stream. Not much, not enough to make him even legally drunk, just enough to show that he had had a couple of drinks that night. Not surprising in someone of Handler's reputation. No traces of any other drugs. The highway safety people or the insurance types might make something of the booze, but I wasn't buying that. Handler probably knew his limit and had been well below it.

That left me only with my nasty suspicions, but at least I had been given the green light by the police to go poking my nose into things. And that meant I could pay a visit on Miss Nielson which suited me just fine

Chapter 3

I had supper at a diner splurging with a fin out of the two hundred dollar advance which was now down to about a hundred and twenty-five and then drove over to Janet Nielson's apartment. If Handler had been footing the bill, he hadn't been a cheapskate. I knew from the papers that one of the other tenants in the building was a former governor. The rent wasn't quite a thousand a month on those places, but it wasn't far off.

The doorman looked askance at me when I parked my Chevy, but when I told him who I was he was polite enough not to mention it. "Miss Nielson is expecting you, Mr. Slade," he said as he opened the inner door and pointed me to the elevator. I could feel his eyes boring into the back of my neck as he made sure I took the car up, but I didn't give him the satisfaction of glancing back at him.

Her apartment was a cozy seven rooms on the tenth floor. It came complete with a balcony and an unobstructed view of the shoreline. It was furnished in what was usually referred to as tasteful elegance.

Not the sort of place you put your feet up on the coffee table while drinking a beer and watching a ball game. She'd probably have beer, but it would be imported from Holland. There wasn't a television set in sight.

She had gotten rid of her mourning dress and was wearing tailored black pants and a blouse of white silk. Janet -- I had decided to call her that at least in my own head -- looked more beautiful than ever. To distract myself I gave the place the once over. There was a piano, grand of course, and a bookshelf full of hard bound books. There were things like Shakespeare and a bunch of German sounding authors. Some of the books were in French. One shelf held what I took to be the complete works of Ezekial O. Handler. The lurid dust jackets looked as out of place as I felt. I wondered if she had read them, but then decided that she had, if for no other reason than her own personal class. There was a picture of Handler on the piano, a blow up of the one that was on the back of all his dust jackets. It had been taken about ten years earlier. I could just imagine a woman like Janet falling for Handler then. Now it didn't really figure, but these days who can tell anything. Maybe he had been a father figure to her.

"I talked to the police," I said, though I felt it was a pretty lame opening.

"What did they say?" she asked anxiously as she took my hat and coat.

"They think it was an accident. There's no evidence otherwise."

"But that means you can keep investigating, doesn't it?" she asked.

"If you still want me to. There wasn't anything suspicious about the car or the autopsy. I don't know if I can find anything out."

"Please, come in and sit down and we can talk. Would you like some coffee? Or a drink?" She seemed awfully eager to please, but then I thought, that had been her job with Handler, hadn't it, to keep the old man happy?

"I'll have a scotch and water if it isn't any trouble."

"No trouble at all. That's what Zeke always used to drink."

She walked over to the liquor cabinet in her tight pants and high heels. I couldn't have helped watching even if I hadn't wanted to. They don't make women like that anymore, I thought. She mixed the drink expertly with smooth, practiced motions. Just right, not too strong. That's a mistake a lot of women make when they want to impress a man. The scotch was a brand that I had heard about but never had. It was sold only in Scotland. She poured a snifter of brandy for herself and then returned with both drinks.

"Did you make a drink for Handler the night he died?" I asked after a first sip of the whiskey. She looked startled and a little bit puzzled. "They found a trace of alcohol in his body," I explained. She looked worried at that. "There wasn't enough in him to make him drunk. He probably only had two or three drinks all night before he died. If I can find out where he had them it might help me to find out where he'd been."

"Oh. Yes, he had one drink here before he left, but that was all. That was probably about seven thirty or eight."

"What time did he leave here?" I asked leaning back on the sofa. Janet had one knee tucked underneath her and was facing me as we talked.

"Just after eight. He said that he had a couple of appointments. People that he had to see. How did you know that he had been here?" she asked. She wasn't defensive like most people would have been. Just curious.

"You were his mistress, after all. I guess I assumed that you were living together. I was wrong about that, wasn't I?" I said, hoping that I hadn't put my foot in it. It was awkward investigating the murder of a man whose mistress I wanted.

"No, Zeke didn't live here. He could be very old fashioned about some things. He didn't live in the past, but he liked things the way they used to be. He had a place on the east side. A big, old mansion. It belonged to one of the old brewery families at one time. It's a huge old place. He lived there with one old housekeeper. I told him that I should just move in there with him instead of having him pay the rent on this place, but he wouldn't hear of it. There was plenty of room and all that, but he said it just wasn't done. I couldn't convince him that it was done all the time. Despite the type of book he wrote, he had something of a romantic nature."

"You've read all his stuff, I suppose?"

"Yes, of course," she said, as if it were unthinkable that she hadn't. Maybe it was. "He was quite good, you know, for a mystery writer. His books aren't all just sex and violence. He had a real way with words, a way of making things sound so realistic that it was like real life. I sometimes think it was too bad that he didn't write serious works, but he said he was a detective writer and that was all."

"He was funny about his writing, too," she went on. The brandy was producing just the hint of a flush on her high, delicate cheekbones and her gray-green eyes looked more animated than I had seen them before. I found myself wishing that she could talk about me and look like that. "He took his writing very seriously, no matter what he might have said about it. He worked very hard on his books. It usually took him about two years to complete one. He could have made a lot more money by just cranking them out. He could have done that, too. But he was always very careful about the details. He wouldn't sell it until everything was just right. He'd never let me see any of his work until he had gotten the proofs back from the printers."

"I'll have to read some of his stuff then sometime," I said, knowing that it sounded like I was trying to make points with her.

"Yes, you must. In fact, I'll lend you one of my copies." She walked over to the bookshelf, looked thoughtful for a moment, and then pulled one of the volumes from the shelf. The title was *The Uncorrupted Corpse.* "I think you'll like this one. It's about a private investigator a lot like you."

I smiled, though my mind wasn't on detective fiction at the time. "Getting back to last night, why don't you tell me what Handler did when he was here last night. I think my best bet in this case is to try and trace his movements up until the time he died."

She nodded seriously, then took my glass to freshen my drink. I thought, if she did much more of that I was going to have to watch myself.

"He stopped by about six thirty. I asked him if he wanted me to fix him supper, but he said that he had already eaten and that he had some things to attend to later. I was to go ahead and fix something for myself. He said he had some typing to do. The second bedroom is set up as a sort of study for him. He often did some work in there while I would fix supper or when he stayed overnight. He was a compulsive worker sometimes."

"He typed for about an hour or so, then he came out and I mixed him a drink. He only had the one. He could drink when he wanted to, but normally he wasn't a heavy drinker."

"He looked worried when he came out of the study, or like a man possessed by a thought. I asked him about it, but he said that it wasn't important, that he was just thinking about a new plot that he had been working on. He said that everything would be all right and that I would be taken care of if anything should happen to him."

"That was one of the things that made me think there might be something wrong with his death. He never had talked that way before. He never seemed to worry about the future. I'd never asked him for anything, no security or anything like that."

"You know that you're the beneficiary of a fairly substantial insurance policy, don't you?" I asked out of habit.

"No, that is I didn't know for sure. I thought it likely

that he had made some provision for me in his will. He had said something about that at one time. He said that if anything should happen to him I was to get in touch with his lawyer. That's all. He didn't really have much of a family, so I guess I wasn't really surprised. He had had a wife at one time, but she divorced him twenty years ago. She's dead now, I think. There weren't any children as far as I know."

"The policy is for a quarter of a million dollars, twice that if his death should be ruled an accident. He took it out just a few weeks ago. I'm not trying to imply anything by that, but that does seem a suspicious coincidence when the man ends up dead within a month. The police or insurance company might try and make something of it. It's the sort of thing their nasty little minds run to."

"You don't mean that they might think that I killed him?" she asked. The way she said it made it seem like the idea had never occurred to her.

"I'm afraid so. Not that they have much evidence to go on. Just don't let it bother you if they should come around asking questions. Tell the truth. Don't try to hide anything, but don't seem too eager, either."

"All right. Thank you for the warning, Frank."

"That's part of what I get paid for," I said, trying to

sound sincere. "You said Handler left here about eight o'clock. Do you have any idea where he was going?"

"He said something about going to the Blue Angel to meet someone. That's a night club on the lower east side. Zeke used to go there occasionally. He took me along a couple of times, but I didn't like it much."

"After that?"

"I don't know. He didn't say anything else. I never pried into his life," she said. She wouldn't, I thought to myself. She was the kind of woman who would accept a man's faults along with the man.

"Is there anything else you can tell me? Anything that might help? Did he have any enemies that you knew of?"

"Not real enemies. He could be loud and even obnoxious at times, but he never really pushed it. Not so anyone would stay mad at him at least. I do know that he was thinking of changing publishers for his new book, and that the current publisher, Ronald Buckley, wasn't too happy about that. If Zeke had signed with someone else Buckler would have lost a great deal of money. A hundred thousand dollars or more. They had an argument about it in a bar one night, but I don't think that Buckley would kill over it. He isn't exactly the violent type. Besides, he's made plenty from Zeke's other books."

"A hundred grand is a lot of money. People get killed every day for nickels and dimes." It sounded hard and cold in that nice warm apartment, but it was true. I didn't know that Buckley character, but I made a note to look him up.

"Well, maybe it's nothing," I said. "Anything else?"

"I don't know if it would be of any use, but he left the pages he had been working on in the study. There might be a clue there. Or at least something to give you an idea of where he was going last night. I'll get them." She walked down the hall to the study. The light went on, but it clicked off a moment later as she reappeared. It hadn't taken her long to find the papers.

"I haven't looked at them, yet. This is just as I found them."

"You didn't even peek? Some people might think your lack of curiosity suspicious," I said.

She blushed at that. It only made her look more beautiful. "I guess it was force of habit. He never wanted me to look at his work before it was published. I just couldn't bring myself to go against his wishes."

She handed me an envelope. It was sealed. I stuck my pocket knife under the flap and opened it. There were three typewritten sheets inside. I started reading the top one:

> I was sitting in my office staring at the frosted glass of the door. It was a cold and rainy Friday morning in October and I had a hangover that made my head feel as faded and peeled as the paint on the walls. The half empty glass of Jack Daniel's wasn't helping my head any, but it was making it easier to ignore some of my other problems. Like how I was going to pay three months back rent on the eight by ten closet the landlord chose to call an office. Jobs had been pretty scarce lately. Even the divorce business had fallen off. No one seemed to care what their spouse was up to anymore. Not for the first time I wondered what the world was coming to.
>
> A sharp rapping sound came that at first I thought was my brain shattering. A second later I realized it was the tap of knuckles on the glass of the door. The lights were off in the office, and it couldn't have looked very promising from the outside, but the knuckles kept up the rapping. Looking through the "evitceteD, EDALS KNARF" printed backwards on the frosted glass I could see the form of the rapper silhouetted by the sixty watt bulb in the hallway. It was a woman, and a good looker by the shadow.

There was more of it, and I glanced through the other pages. It was all there, correct and just as it happened.

"Is this some kind of a joke?" I asked with the anger rising in my voice. I didn't like being played with, not even by a beautiful woman.

"What do you mean?" she asked, the surprise in her voice sounding so genuine that I almost believed her.

"Are you trying to tell me that you didn't write this?" I tossed the pages down on the sofa between us. She picked them up and began to read them. There was a lookof almost horror as she read through the three sheets of paper.

"It's us, in your office. But it can't be. I swear I didn't write this, Frank. These have been sitting on the desk in the study since yesterday evening. They were written at least eighteen hours before we met."

"Do you really expect me to believe that?"

"I don't care what you believe, but it's true," she insisted. "Zeke wrote this. It's his style. The kinds of words he used. It must be some weird, macabre coincidence, Frank. It must be." She was almost hysterical, her icy cool showing cracks.

I wanted to believe her; I wanted to believe that note of desperation in her beautiful voice. It was hard to believe that someone could act that well -- that someone could take me in. I tried to think of explanations, of ways to prove that she hadn't written it herself. I was sure that they had been typed on the machine in the study, but that didn't prove anything. As far as style went, I'd never read anything Handler had written. Even if I had, I wasn't sure that I could have told the difference, not if someone who had read everything he'd ever written, someone who had been intimate with him for years, if someone who knew him as well as anyone could, had wanted to try and imitate him. I would have left then and there, eight hundred bucks, beautiful dame and all, if I could have figured out a reason for her to have dreamed up such a stunt. The trouble was it didn't wash. I couldn't see any motive behind it. That, and I wanted to believe her almost as much as she seemed to want me to.

"Are you sure that this was lying on the desk in the study last night when Handler left?"

"No. I didn't go in there last night. I didn't have any reason to, and Zeke didn't like to have his work disturbed. I didn't go into the study until this afternoon after I had come back from seeing you. That's when I first started acting rationally again and thought he might have left some sort of clue."

"Did you come right back here from my office?"

"No. I had lunch, and then I walked in the park. I

didn't get back here until almost two thirty, I think."

"So someone could have gotten in here and planted this in the time between when you left my office and when you came home?"

"Yes, I suppose so. I was out for almost four hours. But the security in this building is very good. Besides, who could have wanted to do it, and why?"

That was a good question, but I didn't have any answers except the one I didn't want to believe. It was conceivable, just, that someone had witnessed our meeting and then broken into the apartment and written it up in Handler's style. Conceivable, but not believable. There wasn't any logic to it. Not that I could figure out, anyway.

"How many people knew about you? You and Handler, I mean?" Not a nice question, a little blunt, but I was feeling blunt.

"I don't know. We never made a secret of it. But we were never that obvious about it either." She answered, but she was still puzzled and not sure of my attitude towards her.

So we had narrowed it down to the whole world. That line of unreasoning was getting me nowhere fast. I had to change tack, but the pages were still bugging me.

"Why did you pick me to do your investigating, anyhow? I'm not a big time operator or anything. Where'd you get my name?"

"From Zeke. A couple of weeks ago he said that if I ever needed a private investigator I should go to Frank Slade. He said that I could depend on you. Frankly, I didn't know who else to go to when I heard that Zeke had been killed."

Handler's high regard was news to me. I'd met the man, casually, but I would have been surprised if he had remembered my name, let alone recommend me to someone. I don't get many recommendations. Most of the clients treat you like dirt and they're glad to get the whole business over with and never see me again. Usually I feel the same way.

If Janet was lying, I couldn't figure the angle. If she wasn't, I couldn't figure it at all. As much as I wanted to get that dame into the sack, I had to get out of there and do some good, hard thinking.

"Look, it's getting late and I've got a lot of things to check up on tomorrow. I'd better be going." I don't know how sincere I sounded, but she nodded almost reluctantly. I was on the verge of changing my mind and offering to spend the night, but I was just too confused.

She brought me my hat and coat and walked me to the door. "Oh, you've forgotten the book. Read it, please." She went back to the coffee table and picked it up. As an afterthought, she stopped and opened her purse, taking out the eight, crisp one hundreds and stuffing them in the book as bookmarks. She came back and handed me the book, looking as if she wasn't sure I'd take it.

"Thanks," I said. She held out her hand and I took it thinking what a sap I was. Then I opened the door and left.

Chapter 4

I thought about the case on the drive home, but it still didn't figure. I still had no more than a feeling on Janet's part that there was something funny about Handler's death. If I hadn't needed the money and if the Nielson dame hadn't been such a looker, I would have dropped the case. But I had to pay the rent, and the G would just about get me out of hock, not to mention the fact that I still had ideas about Janet. The papers she claimed to have found in Handler's study didn't make any sense at all. I finally gave up thinking and just drove.

I was renting an apartment in a part of town that had been fashionable fifty years earlier. Most of the old mansions had been divided up into apartments long ago, but it was still a nice, quiet location. My place had been the chauffeur's quarters above the garage for one of the old places. It didn't look like much on the outside, or on the inside for that matter, but it had plenty of room for a bachelor, and I didn't have any close neighbors. That can be handy when you keep odd hours.

I parked the Chevy in the garage and went upstairs. I knew before I turned on the light that I wasn't alone. I froze for an instant with my hand at the light switch wondering who might have it in for me. I hadn't worked in so long that I didn't think I had any current enemies. Deciding to brazen it out I flicked on the lights and said hello.

If the character in my easy chair felt any surprise, he didn't show it. I decided right away that we weren't going to get along. He was a fair sized guy in his mid to late forties, a little shorter than me and in good shape for his age. He had the kind of athletic build that comes from squash and tennis courts with maybe some college boxing twenty years earlier. The sort of guy who thinks he can handle anything, but has never been in a drunken brawl with the other fella holding a broken beer bottle. I had been. I'd had a chair in my hand until I broke it over the other guy's head.

He was wearing a dark, three-piece suit that had probably cost more than I had paid for my car. The shoes and shirt were the same level of quality. He had a full head of hair or a really good rug, with just a bit of gray at the temples. I had the impression that if he hadn't grayed naturally he probably would have had it dyed. Distinguished, in a word.

"Are you going to tell me why you moved in, or do I have to get rough?" I asked in my best south side voice.

"I assure you, Mr. Slade, that I have every intention of talking. In fact, that is the purpose of my little visit." He talked smooth like a used car salesman with a Harvard education. Or a politician. I wasn't too keen on either at the time.

"Then you can start by telling me who you are and how you got in." Not a brilliant interrogation, but it was getting late.

"My name is Ronald Buckley. You may have already heard of me. I've been Ezekial Handler's publisher for the last twenty years, but then perhaps Miss Nielson has already told you that?" He paused as if waiting for me to agree or disagree. I did neither. He shrugged and then went on, "As to how I got in, for a man in your profession, Mr. Slade, the security of your household leaves a great deal to be desired. I used a trick from one of Mr. Handler's books to force the lock. One learns something from being a publisher."

"So you're clever, Buckley. If that was all you wanted to tell me you could have dropped me a card and saved us both a lot of trouble." Buckley, with his smooth manner was wearing a little thin. I had enough puzzles for the moment without his butting in.

"I'll get right to the point then. I believe that Miss Nielson has retained you to look into the late Mr. Handler's demise. I would rather you didn't. I am willing to pay you to let the police handle the matter. I'm sure that they are perfectly competent in such things. I have twenty-five hundred dollars here to purchase your disinterest." Buckley laid an envelope on the table with twenty-five crisp C notes in it. For a poor man I was sure seeing a lot of new hundreds lately. Maybe people were just starting to walk around with big wads of cash in their pockets. If so, it would be a boon to the muggers.

"What have you got to hide, Buckley? Twenty-five hundred ain't chicken feed, even to a big time publisher like you." It struck me as a queer deal, but if he thought I might string along, he just might spill something.

"Nothing, Mr. Slade, I assure you. But I do have a business to protect. The amount I have offered you is insignificant compared to what I might make from the sale of Mr. Handler's latest work. I'm just trying to maintain the status quo, shall we say."

"How do you figure? I always thought a little publicity helped sales."

"Publicity, yes. Scandal, no. If you should stir things up too much the papers might find out about Miss Nielson's relationship with Handler. While you and I are both men of the world and understand such things, I'm not sure the public would. They can be very conservative about such things. It's true that sales might pick up for a while, but after the furor died down I believe they might suffer considerably. Handler appealed to a very old-fashioned audience. I have to think in terms of the long run, and I just don't want to take the chance."

I think it was the part about being men of the world that got to me. I'd been to New York and the coast, and the army had put me up at Fort Ord for a while, but that was about as far as I'd gone. But he was still doing the talking, so I decided to play him a little more.

"Well, I don't know much about publishing books, Mr. Buckley, but in my profession when somebody tries to buy you off you tend to get a little suspicious. You didn't have anything to do with Handler's death, did you?"

"No, I didn't," he said with an insincere little smile as though the idea was ridiculous. "I'm sure that it was an accident just as the police are saying. Handler was at my place last night. He had had a couple of drinks, though I wouldn't have called him drunk. Still, the weather was bad. And you know what that road is like. That Jaguar of his wasn't just a toy, you know. He liked to use it. All it would have taken was one mistake. Just slowed reflexes. It could have happened to anyone.

"I'm sure," I said sarcastically. "But it happened to Handler. Miss Nielson told me that he was looking for a new publisher for his next book."

"That may be. Our contract had expired. I'm sure that he was looking for some leverage in our renegotiations. He had come out to my place to discuss the new contract. I had every confidence of resigning him."

"If you are trying to find someone suspicious, Mr. Slade, you might consider your Miss Nielson. I've known Handler for twenty years, but until this last month I'd never heard of this Miss Nielson, though she claims to have been Handler's mistress for some time. Now Handler and I weren't close, socially, but don't you think that I should have at the least heard of her?"

I stared at Buckley. He didn't seem the type that would try a lie like that. It would be far too easy to check on. But it didn't ring true, either. Janet's apartment looked lived in. It takes years to get a place so perfect. She had been too natural, too at ease. One of them was lying. No, not lying. Buckley hadn't made any assertions, he'd just cast a little doubt. He was getting clever, and I was getting tired and confused. I didn't really feel like putting up with any more.

"Look, it's late and I need my sleep. Why don't you get out of here? We can continue our conversation some other time."

"It would be a pleasure," Buckley said, as if I were the flu. "I take that to mean you are refusing my offer.

Well, perhaps it was a mistake on my part. But I trust that you are a man of discretion, Mr. Slade, and will avoid any conversations with the press -- if only in the memory of poor Ezekial."

"Yeah. Poor Ezekial," I said as I handed him his hat and showed him to the door. I shut the door on his back and made sure the dead bolt was shot home. I had been getting careless.

Everything Buckley had said had been plausible. He was a very slick character -- too slick for my taste. Even with the bit about Handler having had a few drinks, but not actually being drunk, he had kept from committing himself. Just enough doubt to throw into question Handler's ability to handle the curves and the fog. The bit about Janet Nielson didn't figure, though, just like a lot of things hadn't been adding up.

I was too confused to sleep, so I got a beer and began to read the book Janet had given me. It was about some down at the heels private dick. I got bored after the first dozen pages. The style did remind me of the three typewritten pages she had found, though. I didn't want to think about it anymore so I went to bed.

I didn't get up until noon the next day. It had been after three when Buckley had left, and I needed my sleep. Not that it had done me much good. I kept having dreams about a giant typewriter typing out the story of my life just before I lived it. I had a slow breakfast of ham and eggs while deciding what to do the rest of the day.

Something Buckley had said about Janet set me to wondering about the woman. She had indicated a lengthy relationship with Handler, but I had never heard of her before. That didn't prove much, but it wouldn't hurt to check up on her. I'd been bit before by clients. I have a suspicious mind, anyway. I'd never found it easy to trust a beautiful dame.

I went back to her apartment building to question the doorman. Usually that's a good source of information. Unfortunately, the one I'd met the night before wasn't there. It was his day off. I talked to his replacement, but he wasn't much help. He'd only been working there a month. He didn't know anything about her except that she had nice legs. I'd already known that.

He did let me in to ask a few questions of the tenants. I'd led him to believe that I was working for the insurance company that had Handler's policy. No one I talked to could remember seeing her before the last month. That didn't mean much. Half of them didn't even know the names of their next door neighbors. In that sort of building people keep to themselves. The rental agent proved a blank. They were closed on Saturdays.

My next stop was the public library. Private eyes aren't supposed to be literate, but you can find out a lot in a library. I read through the social columns in the newspapers for the last three years. Handler's name crept up more than once, but no mention of Janet. But then she wasn't famous and she had said she kept a low profile. It was pretty inconclusive. I hadn't been able to prove that she had existed for more than thirty days, but I hadn't been able to prove the opposite, either. It was a tossup. I decided to give up on that line for the moment and went home to get ready for a night on the town.

Chapter 5

I knew of the Blue Angel by word of mouth, but I'd never been in the place before, at least not under the current name. It was the kind of place that appealed to sensibilities other than my own. I wondered as I drove downtown what sort of attraction the place had had for Handler. He hadn't seemed the type, either. Maybe he had gone there to gather atmosphere for his novels. Maybe he had been slumming. Maybe I'd never find out, but it had been one of the last places he had been seen alive.

The nightclub was located on the lower east side not far from the business district. At one time it had been the bar and restaurant for a fashionable hotel. Now the hotel was an office building and the Blue Angel had taken over the ground floor. The neighborhood wasn't quite seedy, but it wasn't what it had been. Gray-slabbed office buildings and parking garages had taken over and after dark the population dwindled to the tenants of a few rundown apartment houses that hadn't yet faced clearance.

Times had changed, that was for sure, I thought as I parked my car down the street and walked to the club. So had the idea of what constituted a good time. I'd never quite figured out when the change had come, but come it had. The term high society had taken on a different connotation and drugs weren't something reserved for black musicians and crazy boho artists.

The Blue Angel was literally a dive. The bar was entered from a set of steps leading down from the street through a blue painted door sporting a pair of cherubs covered with gilt. Inside the place had been done over in a sort of rococo decadence that was supposed to resemble Berlin before the war. Most of the people in the place hadn't even been born when the Reich fell.

The club had gotten a reputation as being a hangout for what these days they were calling "gays." Not exclusively, for there were plenty of couples that I assumed were heterosexual. The place was also thought of as being risqué, camp, or whatever term was currently in use by the intellectual crowd. There was no doubt that it appealed to those who had money and whose tastes were slightly jaded.

Novelty it offered, I had to grant, if you consider a skinny guy in fish-net stockings and a blonde wig posing as a cigarette girl something new. I turned around and headed for the bar. The bartender wasn't dressed in drag, at least. I ordered a shot of Tennessee sour mash and a bottle of Dutch beer for a chaser.

The show hadn't started yet and things were still

slow at the bar. I motioned the bartender over and asked him if he knew Handler. He gave me a blank stare, but when I pushed over the change from a sawbuck he became more talkative. The writer hadn't exactly been a regular, but he wasn't a stranger to the place, either. He was just enough of a celebrity to have stuck in the bartender's memory.

"Do you remember him being in here the night he had the accident?" I asked above the din of clinking glasses and conversation.

"Thursday night, wasn't it?" the bartender said noncommittally. I ordered another round and laid the change suggestively on the bar. "Yeah, I was working that night. Maybe eight thirty or nine he came in and took a table where he could see the stage. Had a drink, just one I guess. I don't take care of the tables, so I don't remember too well. George does that." George was a guy with curly red hair and high heels. The bartender motioned him over. George looked eager.

"Do you remember seeing Handler talk to anyone?" I asked, stuffing a five down his bodice. "He was supposed to meet someone here. I'm trying to find out if he did."

"No, not that I can remember. No one except Joe, that is."

"Joe?"

"Yeah, Joseph Jaworski, or Josephine LaTouche, rather. He's the star of the show. They talked for a little bit, then Mr. Handler left. That's all I can remember."

As an afterthought he said, "Maybe you'd like to talk to Joe? I might be able to arrange that."

"Yeah, I'd like that," I replied. I passed him another sawbuck which he tucked down next to the five.

"He's about to go on. I'll see if I can get him to talk to you between shows." George left to wait on tables and the bartender had gotten busy at the other end of the bar leaving me to fend for myself. I downed the bourbon in one gulp and started to suck on the beer.

The houselights went down and a piano player started to play. A stacked blonde stepped out into the spotlight and began to sing "Lili Marlene" in a husky voice. Maybe I'm slow, or just old-fashioned, but it took me half a dozen old cabaret songs to realize that the singer was Joseph Jaworski. He didn't have a bad voice, and through the thick blue smoke of the club he didn't look so bad, either. I decided to go gentle on the booze.

The show lasted for an hour with a couple of changes of costumes and some dance numbers. I wasn't quite sure what sex all the performers were. From the looks of most of them they weren't too sure, either.

Finally, the lights came back up. The applause wasn't exactly thunderous, but the audience didn't boo. Maybe it did beat television.

Ten minutes later Jaworski joined me at the bar. He was wearing the sort of tight evening gown that had gone out of fashion with Mae West and Marlene Dietrich. Close up he didn't look too bad, but he wore too much makeup. I've always wondered why guys that like men seemed to make the old femme fatales into cult symbols. I do a lot of wondering. I don't come up with too many good answers, though.

"Want to buy a girl a drink, Mister?" Jaworski asked in a voice that made me think he might be right. He was wasted as a man.

I gave the bartender a sign and he brought a glass over and laid it on the bar taking a fin from the pile in front of me. It was getting to be an expensive evening.

"Thanks, big boy, but you don't look like I'm your type of girl."

"You knew Handler and talked to him Thursday night."

"You a cop?" he asked in a voice suddenly masculine and harsh.

"No, I'm private."

Josephine seemed to relax a bit. "Why do you want to know?"

"His girlfriend doesn't think his death was so accidental. She hired me to find out."

"She never liked me much, but she was always polite about it, at least. Not that I was ever a threat to her. Zeke was very straight. But he never made judgments about anyone, even me. I was sorry to hear he was dead. Do you think he was killed?"

"I don't know. I'm trying to find out. If you talked to him that night it might help me find out."

"He didn't have much to say. He was kind of tense and tired looking. He wouldn't tell me about what. We talked about the show. He said he liked it, but I don't think he watched much of it. He had a couple of sheets of paper on the table and it looked like he had been writing during the show. He was pretty distracted, though. He left them on the table when he went."

"I suppose they got thrown away?"

"No. The busboy saved them and gave them to me. I've got them in my dressing room."

"Could I see them?"

He looked at me strangely for a moment, then laughed resuming the feminine pose. "I think I'll be safe with you."

Josephine led me backstage to the dressing room. In the back the Blue Angel looked like most seedy nightclubs; peeling paint and exposed plumbing. The dressing room odor was a curious combination of perfume and locker room. He picked up a couple of pages from the makeup table litter and handed them to me.

"I've got to get ready for the next show," he said, retiring behind a costume draped screen. I was glad to have the illusion preserved.

I recognized the style at once as Handler's. It was written in a neat script, the kind that isn't taught in schools anymore. The first words caught me, "She had gotten rid of her mourning dress and was wearing tailored black slacks and a blouse of white silk. Janet -- I had decided to call her that, at least in my own head -- looked more beautiful than ever. To distract myself I gave the place the once over."

At first I thought that it was another coincidence, and a plausible one. The woman was his mistress. Why not write about her? But as I read further, the evening I had spent with Janet in her apartment unfolded in front of me again in every detail. It gave me a weird feeling, but the cold, analytical part of my mind reminded me that before I went off the deep end

I wanted to get the handwriting verified as that of Handler's.

But what if it was, that other part of my mind -- the one that was afraid of the dark and things that made night noises – asked? I didn't know. If Handler had written it before he died, he had had some good notion of his impending demise. Also of events that were to take place after his death. That was asking me to believe a lot. If he had known, however, that he was to die, it was easy enough to understand how he might become obsessed about it, even be driven to write about it.

I pulled my imagination back in check. That wasn't the way hardboiled detectives were supposed to think. Still, as I read the sheets over another time I found myself wondering how the characters in Handler's books would react to such a situation.

I gave it up. "Can I keep these?" I asked Josephine.

"Sure, big boy, if you think they'll help." He stepped out from behind the screen in a long red sequined evening gown with black gloves. "Could you zip me up?" he asked turning his back to me.

I did the honors and then got out of there as fast as was polite. There was enough strangeness in my life at that moment without beautiful transvestites. I beat it past the bar and headed out the door. I had gone six steps down the street when a car pulled up at the curb next to me.

"Hey, Slade. Get in," commanded the gritty voice of Lieutenant Flannigan.

"Some other time, Flannigan. I got business to attend to."

"It's about business, Slade. My business. Let's keep it simple and get in the car. I want to take you downtown for some questions."

I shrugged. There was no use arguing with that kind of logic. I got in the back seat. Flannigan sat up front with his driver and neither one did any talking on the way to the station.

Flannigan tossed me a visitor's badge and showed me to an interrogation room. The badge meant that I hadn't been arrested yet. I hoped I could keep it that way.

"You're making waves, Frank," the lieutenant said, some of the tough guy gone now that we were alone. "You're poking into this Handler thing like it was murder."

"Was it?" I leaned back in the hard chair and lit a cigarette. Flannigan glared at me.

"The coroner says it was an accident. There isn't any evidence to show it wasn't." It didn't look like

Flannigan had received any of the notes Handler had been sprinkling around the night he died. I decided that there was no reason he should. "Why can't you just leave it at that, Slade? Play it smart for once."

We were back to tough guy manners and last names again. "If it was an accident, what's the problem with my poking my nose into it a little? Not unless it's still an active murder investigation."

"That's not it, Slade. Handler was a public figure, famous even. If you raise a stink about this one it'll get into the papers big and they'll be saying we're suppressing evidence and conspiracy and who knows what else. The commissioner doesn't want that to happen. We've got enough crime to worry about without that sort of pressure."

"Whose putting pressure on the commissioner? Is it Buckley, Flannigan?"

I could see the light go on in the flatfoot's eyes. I didn't need his denial to know that I was right. I ignored the rest of the lecture and explored the new piece of data. I doubted that Buckley would pull strings with the police commissioner just to save a few bucks. That kind of favor was costly in the long run. He didn't want an investigation, and I could think of only one reason. He had killed Handler. All I had to do was prove it.

I could tell by the silence that Flannigan's lecture was

over. "Look, Flannigan, I'm tired. Either pull my license or let me go home to bed."

"You can go, Slade. But for Christ's sake, keep it clean. There's a lot of weight on this one."

"Yeah, thanks," I said as I headed for the door. Flannigan wasn't above being a nice guy after he had done his duty. I got out of the station fast and caught a taxi to collect my car. It wasn't that late, but I felt tired all of a sudden. I figured I'd found out enough for one night, anyway, and I was going to have a long talk with Buckley in the morning.

When I got home the place reminded me of Buckley's visit the night before. That wasn't the sort of thing I needed on my mind. What I needed was a long legged blonde named Janet Nielson, but I had a lot of things to think about - Buckley, Handler, Josephine LaTouche, and the strange bits of writing Handler had been leaving around. After an hour of trying to sort out the pieces I gave up and went to bed. I dreamt about Janet, but my dreams were interrupted by visions of Janet transforming into Jaworski and of a mad typewriter spewing out pages of a script I had to follow. I woke in a cold sweat. A shot of bourbon finally calmed me down and I fell into a dreamless sleep.

Chapter 6

The weather had been improving and Sunday turned into a beautiful day for a drive, bright and sunshiny. It was the kind of crisp, clear autumn day that makes up for the rest of the year's miserable weather in this part of the country. I decided it would be a nice day to drive up the shore road and maybe drop in on Ronald Buckley while I was in the neighborhood.

I got the Chevy out and headed north, the clean air coming in through the open window helping to clear the muddle out of my head. The sunlight glinted off the waves out on the lake and the trees that lined the road were blazing with fall colors. It was only when I was past the place where Handler had gone off the road that I remembered that the purpose of my drive was to visit Buckley. It was a shame, because it was a damn good day for a drive.

I had made up my mind about the case. Buckley had iced Handler for business reasons, i.e. a loss of a percentage on Handler's new book. I knew that I didn't have any proof, but it felt right. I'd learned to trust my feelings. You have to in this kind of business. The other things - Handler's little missives, his connection with the fag, Jaworski, even the slightly mysterious past of Janet Nielson - those were all irrelevancies to the murder. It was hard to think of Janet as irrelevant.

Buckley had done it. All I had to do was prove it. It didn't matter that I didn't know the method. I would find that out in time. Buckley was worried about me. All I had to do was put a little pressure on him, make him start to sweat. If I did that, he'd crack. He was half way there, already. All he needed was a little push.

I almost missed his place. There wasn't anything to see from the road except a mailbox and a twist of asphalt driveway leading up the hill into the trees. I had to stop the Chevy and back up. There wasn't any gate to stop me, just the mailbox by the side of the road, so I drove up the driveway and parked next to the big, black Mercedes. The house wasn't big, not a mansion, but it went along with the expensive German sedan. It was one of those California style places, all natural wood and glass with a lot of crazy angles and odd bits sticking out. It fit in with the trees and even from the drive I could see that the living room had a hell of a view.

I didn't know what to expect when I rang the doorbell, a butler, or what. It was Buckley that answered. From what I saw he was alone. At least there was no one in the living room after he invited me in. I had been right about the view. The lake just faded into nothingness in the distance. If the place was what publishing had gotten him I could see why he might kill to hang on to it.

"What can I do for you, Mr. Slade?" Buckley asked politely.

"Last time we met I said I might have some more questions. I do, so I came to ask them."

He didn't seem surprised. Instead, he sat down in a Scandinavian style leather chair and looked bored. There was no response for a moment. Then he said, "Well?"

"For one, what time did Handler get here that night?"

"I'd say about ten, or a little after. Does it matter?"

"It might. I've traced his movements that night until about nine thirty. That leaves just about enough time for him to drive up here. As far as I can find out he'd only had two drinks before he got here. Not really enough to make a man drunk. Not a man like Handler."

"I quite agree, Mr. Slade. He had another drink here, a whiskey and water, but it wasn't particularly strong. I don't think that he finished it either. He wasn't drunk, but he wasn't sober, either. If his reflexes were slowed down just a little, it would have been enough under those conditions."

"Perhaps," I said. Buckley was playing it cool, not

claiming anything, not saying anything that could be refuted. But I could sense a certain edginess underneath. He'd crack alright, and that civil exterior would split apart. I'd have him then. Or he'd have me. I reminded myself that despite his politeness he'd already killed one man.

"The police said that Handler went into the lake around eleven. What time did he leave here? Was there time enough for him to have stopped anywhere else?"

"He left about then. Eleven, I mean. The place where he had the accident is about five minutes from here. If he crashed when you say he did, then I don't think that he could have stopped anywhere else unless it was at one of my neighbors, and then only for a second. There isn't anything else on this stretch of road."

"He didn't stay long, did he? It hardly seems worth his trouble. It took me nearly half an hour to get here from my place. It must have been longer that night, say forty-five minutes, at least. Yet he only stayed for about that same length of time. He must have had important business to take that much trouble on a night like Thursday."

"Not so important. Ezekial was a very direct sort of man, Mr. Slade. He liked to confront people. He also liked to drive that sports car of his. His behavior that night was in no way out of the ordinary."

"That's strange. Someone who saw him just before he came up here said that he was behaving just that, out of the ordinary. He seemed preoccupied with something. I was hoping you might be able to tell me what?"

"I'm afraid not," he said smoothly. He was beginning to relax. I hadn't asked him any tough ones. He was enjoying playing with me.

"Well, what did he come up here to talk to you about?"

"Just some details of the contract on his new book. He had some questions. I answered them and then he left. That's all. Nothing mysterious."

"Would you mind telling me exactly what those details were?"

"As a matter of fact, I would mind, Mr. Slade. It's really none of your business." He said it politely, but there was a hint of nastiness underneath his voice.

"Then maybe you could tell me why you had the commissioner put pressure on me to keep out of this case?" The nastiness in my voice was more than a hint.

"You're trouble, Slade. I don't want that. You weren't amenable to my offer so I decided to take other measures. I haven't finished, either."

"It seems like a lot of trouble over a dead author. Or do you have something else to hide?" I let the last word hang like an implication. He knew that I was a threat to him. A man like Buckley isn't used to threats. He thinks he can take care of himself, but he never really has to. I had him back on edge again, and that was good.

"Look, Slade," he said, his voice rising, "I don't know what your game is, but don't try anything with me. Handler had an accident, and that's that. You can't prove otherwise and you aren't going to get anything out of me to make you keep out of it. There are laws in this state against blackmail, and I have some powerful friends."

"Who said anything about blackmail, Buckley? I thought we were talking about murder."

That got to him for a moment, like cold water from a bucket. He got very cool again after that, but I knew that I had him. It wouldn't take much more. Just a shred of proof would be enough.

"There's been no murder, Slade. Just a two-bit attempt at blackmail. I checked up on you. You're about as phony as that Nielson woman. Your investigator's license is real, but just about everything else is a lie. According to everything that I checked, before a month ago you didn't even exist.

No one ever heard of you. No one saw you in your apartment. No one remembers your office. Just like Miss Nielson. You both seem to be lacking a past. Do you think that you can bear close scrutiny, Mr. Slade? I'm on to you and that woman. You won't get anything out of me. If anyone is going to get into trouble, it'll be the two of you. Now get out of here."

"What's that supposed to mean?"

"Come off it, Slade, or whatever your real name is. Who did you expect to fool with your parody of a private eye? Look at yourself. You could be a gumshoe out of one of Handler's novels. You're twenty-five years out of date. No one is like you anymore. The tough guy you're trying to play is as archaic as Phillip Marlowe. The same goes for that Nielson woman. You're both out of the past, images from one of Handler's hack pieces. If you wanted to try blackmail you could at least have brought your characters up to date. I've had enough of this charade. You aren't getting anything out of me. Now get out."

He pointed at the door with a theatrical gesture. I picked my hat up off the coffee table and left. I was confused again. Not about Buckley being the murderer. I still believed that. But his reaction had thrown me. I had thought that he might explode if I pushed him. In fact I had been hoping for that. Instead he had accused me of not existing.

On the drive back I got to wondering whether Buckley was insane. Maybe that was the reason he had done in Handler. He couldn't seriously believe that I didn't exist, that I was just somebody playing a part. Not if he was sane. But if he had a paranoid delusion that there was some sort of plot against him his accusations might be more believable.

He had made the same sort of accusations about Janet. I had checked on her, though. I hadn't been able to find any firm evidence of her existence going back more than a month. Not anything conclusive, but it had looked suspicious. Could Buckley have had the same trouble with me. It didn't seem possible that in this day of computer records and government regulations that a person's past could disappear, but maybe it could. A chill ran up my spine. What proof did I have that I actually had existed more than a month ago? It was a good question.

I didn't drive home. Instead, I went to the office. There was some mail from the Saturday delivery that had fallen through the slot and onto the floor. I ignored it and got the bottle out of the drawer. I was beginning to wonder if Buckley's paranoia was contagious. He had raised the question of my own existence and the more I thought about it, the more it bothered me. All the way back to the office I had tried to think of tests that would prove the reality of my past. They weren't very satisfying, not to someone as suspicious as I am.

I had my memories, but they existed in the present. They didn't prove that I had actually existed in the past; they just proved that I thought that I had. The same went with all my papers, driver's license, P.I. ticket, the works; except that they proved that someone else thought that I had lived in the past - that is, if they were genuine.

I'm not much of a philosopher. I needed action. I started to make some phone calls. It was pretty strange, asking questions about myself. I got some pretty strange reactions, too, from the people I called.

Four hours later I had hung up the phone. I had asked plenty of questions, but I wasn't sure that I liked the answers. One thing I had discovered. Not many people knew me, not closely, not close enough to tell me that they had known me last year or five years ago or ten. Plenty of people knew of me, knew I was a private detective, but anything more than that and their memories got a little hazy. I had had trouble getting a hold of old clients. They all seemed to have moved or be out or something. Not necessarily strange considering some of them, but disconcerting when I wasn't able to find one of them that I had worked for more than a month ago. In the end, the only person with a recollection of me had been Flannigan. He knew me well enough, not that he had been happy with my interrupting of his football game with crazy questions.

That only started me wondering. I called a couple of more people and asked them about Flannigan. I got the same sort of answers about him as I had about myself and Janet. No outright denials, but no strong, positive reactions, either. That was when I decided to stop making phone calls. I also decided to finish the bottle of bourbon sitting on my desk.

Chapter 7

Later, I wasn't sure how much later, the phone jangled irritatingly on the desk. The office was dark and only a finger of bourbon remained in the bottle. I let the phone ring half a dozen times until it stopped. There wasn't any point in my answering it, I thought. After all, I didn't really exist.

A moment later the phone began to ring again with its monotonous six second rhythm. It was more insistent this time. After the tenth ring I fumbled across the desk in the dark and answered it tipping over my glass in the process. It didn't really matter. The glass was empty.

"Frank?" the soft, sensuous voice of Janet Nielson asked from the earpiece. "Frank, are you all right?"

I was touched that she might be concerned about me, but then people that didn't exist had to stick together. "Yeah. I'm okay, jes' a little drunk, that's all." It wasn't the way to make an impression on a woman like Janet. I doubted that Handler had ever slurred his words no matter how drunk he had been.

"Can you come over right away?" There was an urgency in her voice that went a long way towards sobering me up.

"What's wrong?"

"I don't want to talk about it over the phone, but it's important. Will you come? Please?"

I'm not sure I could have ignored her pleading even if she hadn't been beautiful. "I'll be over in ten minutes, okay? Just have some black coffee ready for me."

"Thanks, Frank," she said before hanging up. Those last words had been almost a caress.

My own troubles were forgotten. I grabbed my coat and headed for the door, but as I reached it I noticed the mail on the floor. Most of it was bills and junk, but there was a manila envelope big enough to contain a handful of typewritten sheets. There wasn't any return address, but the postmark was dated Thursday afternoon. On a hunch I stuffed it into my pocket and left.

It was seven minutes, not ten, when I parked my car outside Janet's apartment building. There was a different doorman on duty. He gave me the fisheye, but passed me up. The elevator ride seemed to take forever. The adrenalin generated by Janet's phone call was starting to wear off and my legs were feeling shaky from the bourbon.

She was waiting at the door for me. The doorman must have warned her. It was the kind of thing that doormen do in those kinds of buildings when they see a low class drunk stumble in through the front door. She was dressed simply in a gray wool skirt and a high necked sweater that looked like it was probably cashmere. She was in her stocking feet and her blonde hair was pulled back into a knot at the nape of her neck. She was still beautiful.

She looked disapprovingly at me, but I had the impression it was my condition and not my person that she disapproved of. She stood at the doorway for a moment as if she were deciding whether to say something. I moved past her and dropped on the couch, glad to be off my feet.

"Do you have the coffee ready?" I asked. She bit her lip and nodded, going in to the kitchen. She brought out two cups and a pot on a tray. There was cream and sugar on the tray, but I didn't use any. The coffee was black and strong and I started to feel better. I could feel her close to me, watching. She was on the couch beside me, with her legs tucked underneath her. She had lost her composure, something she hadn't done before, not even in my office the morning after Handler's death.

"I'm okay, now," I said to reassure her. For some reason that seemed to help. "What was it that you couldn't tell me over the phone?"

"Ronald Buckley was here this afternoon. He wasn't very pleasant. He seems to think that I am trying to blackmail him. He said that I had hired you to prove that he had killed Zeke so he would pay us off to keep from going to the police."

"I am trying to prove it, because he did it. I can't, yet, but he killed him." From her reaction it looked as though the idea was new to her.

"It wasn't an accident, then?" she asked.

"No, it wasn't, but I can't prove that yet, either." I still didn't have any idea how Buckley had done it. "Buckley's getting nervous. He knows that I'm on to him. Don't let him worry you, but if he bothers you again, tell me."

"That's not all, Frank," she said uncertainly. "He said some strange things - things I didn't understand. The implications are pretty unsettling. He accused me of not being me, that I was an imposter, that I was playing the part of Ezekial's mistress so that I could extort money from him. Buckley, that is. He was adamant about it. He said that he could prove that no one had ever heard of a Janet Nielson before last month. He said that if I didn't make you drop the investigation he would go to the police and claim that I was blackmailing him."

"They'll laugh at him. He can't prove a thing."

"I'm not so sure," she said.

"What do you mean? You've been Handler's mistress for some time, haven't you?"

"Yes, of course, but I'm not sure that I can prove it. The apartment is in Zeke's name. He had it before I met him. I don't think that I'm the first woman who's lived here. We never made a secret of our relationship, but we didn't go out much where people would notice me." I raised my eyebrow at that and she smiled.

"I know that I'm attractive, but Zeke was the celebrity, not me. I always stayed in the background when we were in public. We both liked it better that way. The fact is, I'm not sure that I can prove in a court of law that I have been his mistress for the last two years, or that I've even been in this city at all during that time. I don't really have any friends. I don't have a job. I'm afraid that I'm not even registered to vote." She finished with a helpless sigh that I could understand. I had already gone through the same thing. Her reaction to it had been better than mine. I had tried to wrap myself around a bottle of bourbon.

"Look, there's no sense worrying about this right now. Buckley intimated something like this to me a couple of days ago. He's been pretty clever about this whole thing. Anyway, I spent a little time checking up on you."

There was a flash of anger at that, and then she relaxed seeing my reasons. "You can prove that I've been around for a couple of years?"

"No. I couldn't prove anything one way or another, but that means Buckley can't prove anything, either. Certainly not enough to get the D.A. to do anything about it. The law doesn't like to look foolish."

"But the possibility exists? That Buckley could fabricate something and get me arrested?" She was worried, but I didn't think that it was the threat of arrest that bothered her. It was her reality.

"If it will make you feel better, Buckley tried to pull the same stunt on me. He sounded sure enough of himself that I spent time checking myself out. I didn't have much better luck than I did with you. Only some character references of dubious merit. It's easy to be anonymous in the kind of society we've got these days."

She nodded, and then smiled, extending her hand to my shoulder. I reached up to grasp the smooth fingers. "If he tries to pull anything you've always got a detective to prove you're real." She gave me a look that made me want to melt, a look of trust. I wasn't used to that kind of look from a woman, not one that was sober, anyway.

"I got something in the mail yesterday. I think it may be from Handler." I pulled the envelope from my pocket and explained about the pages Handler had left at the Blue Angel. There were three typewritten sheets inside the envelope. They had been typed on a different machine than the one in the study, but the style was definitely Handler's. We read the pages together, Janet moving closer so that her shoulder pressed against mine.

The scene described was Janet's apartment. We were both there going through the papers in the study. It ended with us finding a notebook and opening it. Maddeningly, that was it.

"What do you think?" I asked her when we were done.

"Zeke wrote that, I'm sure. But the other two parts, they were about things that had already happened, weren't they?"

"When we read them they had, but they both must have been written before the event. Maybe we just read this one early."

"You don't really think that Zeke had some way of seeing into the future, do you?" Janet asked, the uncertainty back.

"I don't know what to think. Maybe it's a hoax. Or a coincidence. This whole business has been strange. But I think that we have to go look in the study and see if we can find the notebook."

She nodded agreement and got to her feet unfolding her beautiful legs from underneath her. I put my arm around her waist. She didn't resist, but led the way to the study.

The study wasn't a big room. It had originally been intended as a second bedroom. There was a big desk against one wall underneath a window, an overstuffed easy chair and a reading lamp, and a bookcase next to the desk. It was furnished simply in contrast to the rest of the apartment, a place to work without distractions.

Once inside the room, Janet seemed reluctant to continue the search. Handler had kept the room off bounds and she still felt the power of his personality in the study. I could, too, and it wasn't just the smell of cigar smoke. I've never felt any respect or fear of the dead, though, not when I needed to satisfy my curiosity.

The search of the desk proved fruitless. There was a typewriter, a box of typing paper, a cup holding a pen and a couple of pencils, a dictionary, and thesaurus. None of it was out of the ordinary for a writer. The drawers weren't locked, but all they yielded were some more pencils, another box of paper, one of paper clips, and a used typewriter ribbon. The bottom drawer had a couple of notebooks in it, but they only contained some notes for possible plots. They didn't seem worth the buildup of Handler's latest message.

I turned my attention to the bookcase. Janet was closer now, looking over my shoulder as I knelt to examine its contents. The first shelf held references, an atlas, another dictionary, a book on small arms. Some mysteries filled the second shelf, all by other writers. The books on the bottom shelf were stranger and seemed out of character. They were mostly about magic and the occult. I remembered what Armand O'Hara had said about Handler buying occult magazines. Maybe he had been doing research for a book, but some of the volumes looked old and they seemed to have been used a lot.

"Was Handler really into this stuff?" I asked.

"He never said anything about it to me," Janet replied. "He was the type of man who was interested in things that were real. He wasn't the least bit superstitious. There was never anything supernatural in any of his books, either." She paused and then added after a moment's thought, "It does seem strange, doesn't it?"

"Yeah." I was getting used to weird things on this case, but if Handler was fascinated by the occult it was odd that he hadn't betrayed himself to her. She felt that way, too. I could sense a bit of distance coming between her and the memory of the man she had loved.

There didn't seem to be any notebook in the bookcase, but as I was about to straighten up I saw that one book on the end bulged oddly, it's binding broken. I pulled it from its place and it folded open revealing a pocket-sized spiral notebook. There was a chill down my spine and I knew that this was the notebook that Handler had written about.

There were only about twenty pages in it. The rest had been torn out, and what remained were still caught in the coil of the binder. Thumbing through it, the last dozen pages were blank; each of the rest had a name at the top followed by some notes. I started over, this time reading from the front.

The heading of the first page was Armand O'Hara. A brief but accurate description led the notes and then some comments on his career and accident. It was the sort of prose sketch an author might use to describe a character in a book. At the bottom was the date August 12 and the single word, success.

Janet looked at me quizzically. "Armand is a newsboy near my office. Handler used to buy magazines there occasionally. Buckley's office is within walking distance, too. I guess that was why Handler was in the neighborhood," I explained.

I flipped the page and saw Janet's name. The pattern followed the first page, but the description was much more detailed and quite flattering, but at the same time it was surprisingly objective. Not the way a man would normally describe his mistress. There was also a description of the apartment, also very explicit. There was another date at the bottom of the entry which ran over two pages. It was September the third.

I noticed that Janet was blushing and I smiled. The entries didn't make any sense to me, but then I wasn't a writer. It looked as if Handler had been taking notes to model characters after people he knew.

The name on the next page I turned caught my attention. It was dear old Lt. Flannigan's. I wondered how he had managed to crop up in Handler's book of tricks. The cop had never said anything about having met the writer. They weren't likely to travel in the same sort of circles, either. Again there was a date, the twelfth of September.

The next page described Joseph Jaworski, alias Josephine LaTouche. The date was the 30th. The last three entries hadn't had any comment after the date. Handler seemed to have proved his point, whatever it was, after Armand.

I turned to the last entry pretty sure of what I'd find. That didn't stop the goose bumps when I saw my own name at the head of the page. The description was accurate if not flattering. I wasn't sure that I liked being described as a hardheaded gumshoe who drank too much. There were descriptions of my apartment and my office, though Handler had never been to either place, at least not while I had been there. There couldn't have been any mistaking of either place from the descriptions. He had them both down to the cockroaches and peeling paint. It was a spooky feeling reading about myself like that. I didn't like the idea of Handler knowing so much about me.

The date at the bottom of the page was the fourth of October, the day Handler had died. There was a note, too, "it's done." After that, nothing except for a scribble on the facing page, "F.S. see home library. Z.H."

There was one name missing, one that I had expected, and that was Ronald Buckley's. Everybody else that I had run across in the case, everyone who had had any part to play at all had been in the notebook. But not the publisher. It broke the pattern, but I wondered if that was because he was the murderer.

The dates didn't seem to follow any pattern, either, except as a sequence leading up to the day of the murder. The notes might have served as a reference for the pages Handler had been leaving around, but I had a feeling that it went beyond that.

I looked up at Janet. I could see that she was as puzzled as I was, but she seemed to be expecting some comment. "It beats me," I said with a shrug. "I can't figure it out, not so as to make any real sense. It sure looks like Handler knew he was going to get bumped off, and that he wanted me to investigate, but I can't figure this stuff out at all."

"What about the last entry, 'F.S. see home library?' It's written in a different ink, and not neatly like the rest."

"I don't know." I wasn't feeling very bright.

"Those could be your initials, and 'see home library' could be instructions to look for something in the library at his house."

"Yeah, it could be," I said lamely. At that moment I wasn't sure that I wanted to find any more clues. I was getting a funny feeling about the way that they were adding up.

"I've got a key. We could go over and check it out," Janet said with determination. She wanted to find out in a bad way. I hoped she wouldn't mind the answer too much.

I knew that we had to go whether I liked it or not. We had both gone too far to turn back. The chain was pointing to that library and the game had to be played to the end.

"Okay, give me the key. I'll check it out."

"I'm coming too," Janet said. For a moment I thought of refusing, but I couldn't.

"Grab your coat, then."

Chapter 8

She drove us over to Handler's mansion. She handled the small German sedan well. I spent the time admiring her slim, firm hands and long smooth legs, trying not to think of what we might find in the library.

The house was as she had described it, a huge old mansion of brick built in a style that couldn't decide whether it was Victorian, Georgian, or classical. It was set well back behind a wall and a yard of tall, foreboding oaks. It wasn't at all the kind of place to visit on a cold, windy autumn night, not even with a warm, beautiful woman on the seat next to you.

She parked in front of the garages and used her key on the side door. Janet knew her way around the place because she found the light switch without searching. The dim bulb in the ceiling didn't do much to dispel the gloom of the house. It just made it seem bigger and emptier.

"The housekeeper must have left," Janet said, taking my hand in hers. "That's probably just as well. She never cared much for me." I was glad of it, too. Technically we weren't breaking and entering, but it wasn't something that I'd want to put to a test.

The inside of the house was as one would expect. There was lots of dark, wood paneling and brass fixtures. The place showed its age. I could see where the gas outlets had been taken out and replaced with electric lights. From what I could see, a lot of the house hadn't seen much recent use. I wondered why Handler had kept living there. Maybe the mood had helped him write. It was the sort of place where one could imagine murder easily.

The library, when Janet had led me there, was in scale with the rest of the house. It had been built to hold ten or twenty thousand books, and Handler had filled up most of the shelves. I wasn't sure what it was that we were supposed to find, if anything, so I walked around the room glancing at the titles of books. There were some that I recognized, a lot more that I didn't -- classics, novels, references, books on law and medicine. Most of them were old, twenty or thirty years at least. It was a random collection. They looked as if Handler had bought them by the pound from a used bookstore just to give the place atmosphere.

As I was looking, Janet had been poking through the papers on Handler's desk. I continued my inspection. One thing intrigued me, an old bookcase with glass doors. The doors were locked when I tried them, but I could read the titles through the panes. They were all on magic and witchcraft, hundreds of them, and not the sort of thing one picked up at an ordinary bookshop. Most of them were old, nineteenth century and earlier, big books bound in leather with the titles in gold, small books bound in cloth. They weren't all in English, either. I knew enough to recognize Latin and Greek and something that I thought was probably Hebrew. Handler had been serious about the stuff, that was clear. It had taken a great deal of time and money to amass the collection. Crackpot junk or not, those books were rare and expensive, and very hard to find.

Janet called me away, clutching a stack of typing paper in her hand. I didn't doubt that it was another piece of the story written by Handler. Silently she handed the sheets over to me and I sat down in one of the overstuffed leather chairs and began to read:

> As I opened Buckley's desk drawer I knew that I had found the final piece of the puzzle, the one thing that had eluded me, the murder weapon. I had never really doubted that Buckley was guilty. He had been too interested in keeping me from investigating. Handler's decision to look for another publisher, and I was sure that that had been his intention, had provided the motive. Ten percent of a million was a lot of incentive.
>
> All I needed was the proof, and that lay before me in the drawer. I had what I needed, what I could go to the cops with. Suddenly, all the weird parts of the case, the notes from

Handler, his premonitions of his own death, his occult interests were unimportant. It didn't even matter that I couldn't prove that I really existed, or prove that Janet did either. I had a job to do, and that was to get the goods on Buckley. I had promised Janet that I would do that much, and now I had what I needed.

The first page of the stack ended with no further explanations. I read the other pages, but they were of no help. They told of my driving up to Buckley's place and breaking in. Handler had evidently written these last pages in a hurry and left them stacked in the order they had come out of the typewriter.

I was still in the dark. If Handler had known how he was going to be killed he hadn't seen fit to make my life any easier. Maybe he hadn't known either, but that didn't make any sense. Not, that is, if I accepted his omniscience so far. I was as confused as I had been.

If Handler had written all the clues, how had he known what would happen? Had it been a lucky guess? Or had Handler's interest in the occult paid off. Could he in some way read the future, and in doing so had he seen his own murder? If he had, why hadn't he been able to avert it? To call in a second rate P.I. after the fact seemed a complex way of arranging one's affairs.

Suddenly I wasn't buying it. That sort of thing didn't happen, not in real life. There weren't any crystal balls or voices from the dead. I didn't know who had written all the pieces, and I didn't know why. I didn't know why I hadn't been able to trace my past, either. What I did know was that I was being used. For some reason that I couldn't understand, I was being maneuvered. My best guess was that it was part of some plan of Buckley's to protect himself by pinning the murder on someone else, either Janet or myself.

I didn't like it one bit. It stunk. The question was, what was I going to do about it? I didn't seem to have much choice. Somebody wanted me up at Buckley's place that night. I'd be happy to oblige them, but they were going to find that I had a few surprises in store for them.

My mind had taken a nasty turn and it must have showed to Janet. "Frank, what are you going to do?"

"What do you think? I'm going up to Buckley's. There doesn't seem to be much else to do. If that's where the murder weapon is, I've got to find it before I can prove anything. As it is, I don't even know what it is."

"I'll go with you," she said strongly.

"Not this time, babe. It's too dangerous. I don't

want to have to worry about you." I was starting to worry about her, all right, but not in the way I was leading on. She argued some more, but finally broke down and gave me the keys to the sedan.

I stopped by the office to get a gun, a magnum revolver that made fist sized holes in whatever it hit. It's weight in my coat pocket made me feel better, a lot better.

I had sobered up by then and the wheels were racing around inside my head like the engine of the German sedan as I drove it up the shore road towards Buckley's. The pieces were falling in place, the important ones at least. I went over them again and again, working it all out. The big thing was that Handler was dead, and that I had been hired to find the murderer. There were no doubts about either of those facts. If Handler was dead, he wasn't the one who had been playing games with me. Buckley had, that was sure. Flannigan and LaTouche figured as bit players. So did O'Hara, if he had had any part to play at all.

The chunks of story weren't so hard to figure anymore. Someone, either Buckley or Janet had written them. Both had been close enough to Handler to counterfeit his style, at least enough to fool a gumshoe like myself. The first one could easily have been written after the fact, after Janet had visited my office. The second one might or might not have been written in advance, depending on where LaTouche figured into things. Either way, it wouldn't have been too hard to figure out. They'd have known that I'd show up at her place sooner or later. It could have been staged to match the script. The last two had been read before the events had happened, but because of that they had become self fulfilling predictions. Nothing was mysterious about any of it. The occult books were just a blind or window dressing to confuse me. One thing was certain, Janet was a party to it all. I didn't like that idea. I had fallen for her, fallen in a big way. But that wasn't going to stop me from doing my job.

The moon was full, and the white light danced off the waves on the lake below. The trees that had looked so glorious in the sunlight now took on a sinister aspect, the wind whipping denuded branches so that they cast eerie silhouettes. I parked the car up the road from Buckley's and cut through the woods up to the house. It was cold, almost freezing and I turned the collar of my coat up around my neck.

There weren't any lights on in the house and the Mercedes wasn't in sight. It looked as if I was in luck and Buckley was gone. I checked the gun in my right pocket and the small flashlight in my left. Both were there to reassure me. It had been a long climb up the hill to the house and I was winded. I rested for a moment, casing the place. There wasn't any movement so I moved in.

I decided to break the script. The pages had said

that I would use the back door to get in. I tried a window in one of the bedrooms. A little knife work allowed me to remove the screen. The storm window and inside glass slid up easily, almost noiselessly. That made me smile, a little triumph over whoever had been directing my life.

I swung myself in through the window using a short flick of the flash to catch my bearings. The door of the room was open. Through it I could see moonlight shining into the living room. I didn't need the flash anymore to find my way. I slid it back in my pocket, but drew out the revolver.

I didn't know my way around the house. I hadn't seen anything but the living room on my last visit, but it didn't take long to find the study and Buckley's desk. The drawer was there, too. I slid it open and used the flash to examine its contents. I was disappointed. I didn't see anything that looked like a weapon, at least nothing that could have killed Handler the way he had gone.

I set my gun down on the top of the desk and rummaged around. That was a mistake. I heard a click and the lights went on. My hand went for the gun, but it never made it. It stopped when I found myself looking down the barrel of a .38 automatic.

The gun was in Buckley's hand. "Looking for this, Mr. Slade?" he said in the same irritatingly polite tone that he always used. In the hand that didn't hold the gun he held a small vial of clear glass, the kind of thing medicine comes in. I didn't know what it was, but I could guess. It was something that he had put in Handler's drink, and it had caused him to drive off the cliff into the lake.

"Could be," I said, wondering what my chances were of going for my gun. They weren't good enough. Not by a long shot. Buckley had a kind of crazy look in his eye. He'd be all too willing to shoot.

"That's unfortunate, because I'm not going to let you have it. I don't want you to try anything foolish, so why don't you move away from that big gun of yours and have a seat. Over there, the chair in front of the desk where I can watch you while we chat." He motioned with the gun. I sat where he pointed. He sat, too, in the desk chair, setting the vial next to my revolver. He kept the gun in his hand pointed at me.

"For your information, that vial contains what killed Ezekial. Nothing poisonous, you understand. In fact, it's a rather harmless drug, an antihistamine, I believe. Very effective in small doses, if you have hay fever, that is. Of course it does have one small side effect. It inhibits hand-eye coordination, especially in the presence of alcohol. Fast acting, too. It only takes a half hour to work."

I sat impassive, though it figured. I wasn't going to give Buckley any satisfaction. He didn't seem to like that. He wanted an audience. He continued, anyway. "Clever, I should think. The sort of thing you should appreciate. Professionally, that is. No? Perhaps it's too subtle for your taste. But not for mine. I just gave him a little bit. Just enough to throw his driving off. That's one of the things the warning label says. But the dosage was small. Not the sort of thing that they'd pick up in a routine analysis. Not unless they knew what they were looking for. And they wouldn't. I made sure of that."

"They never will, either. I shall destroy this presently. I shouldn't have kept it this long. A mistake, I suppose. But one that I can correct. Then it will be a secret between just the two of us." He looked at me quizzically. "Yes, that's right. Between the two of us. I'm not going to kill you, Mr. Slade. That might attract too much attention. But if I dispose of this it won't matter. You'll have no proof. It will be your word against mine. They won't find anything in Handler's body, either. Not after this long. The drug degrades rather rapidly."

I was pretty sure that he had the right of it. I couldn't prove anything. Without the vial I probably couldn't even prove that there had been a murder, let alone that Buckley had done it. Buckley could see the defeat written on my face. He smiled. He gloated. I wanted to kill him. He had the gun.

He was in a talkative mood. "A curious thing happened today. After you left I received a package by messenger. It was from Ezekial. It contained an extraordinary story. It accused me of killing him. It even had the method right. Ezekial claimed in it that he had divined it all in some occult way. He had been dabbling in that stuff for some time. Not many people knew that, but I did. Not quite the image he presented to the public. Personally, I think that he was getting senile. Poor Ezekial longed for the good old days when men were hardboiled and the women soft and pliant. Rather like yourself and Miss Nielson, I imagine."

The publisher was rambling. I wasn't too sure that he was sane. I was also wondering if in some schizophrenic way he had written the clues while suppressing conscious knowledge of the fact. Maybe out of guilt. It wasn't the kind of psychology that I was up on, but it might figure.

"That wasn't the extraordinary part, though. He claimed in his note that he had created you, conjured you up as a golem to avenge his death. You and Miss Nielson and assorted minor characters. An interesting delusion, isn't it? His claim was that he evoked you through the power of his writing. He just wrote you down and you appeared by some magic."

"It's the sort of thing you might expect from Handler. He always did think too much of his writing ability. This is just the ultimate vanity. Personally I've always found his writing too florid, too descriptive for my tastes." Buckley paused, and my theory seemed more plausible. I could see the hate that he had had for Handler, a pathological kind of hate.

"Of course, it might be true," the publisher said. "An interesting thought, isn't it? Then you wouldn't really exist. You'd just be a figment of Ezekial's imagination, the last echoes of his much vaunted creativity. That could explain your mysterious lack of a past, and Miss Nielson's, too."

The thought brought me up cold. There was a hint of truth in it. I had convinced myself that the pieces of the plot were the works of a guilty madman, or part of his plan to avert suspicions from himself. But the doubts were all coming back. Janet, Flannigan, Armand O'Hara, Josephine LaTouche. They all seemed like characters out of a book, out of the type of detective stories that Handler had written. Even myself. The hard drinking, hard boiled private eye. I realized how much of an anachronism we all were. How out of place we seemed. Especially myself.

"Ah, but you take the idea too seriously, Mr. Slade. Such things don't happen, not in the real world." The mystical look had gone out of his eye. Now he just looked crazed and ready to kill. "It's much more likely that this was all a device of Miss Nielson and yourself to blackmail me. Very elaborate and certainly imaginative."

"You show disbelief. Well, perhaps you weren't in on

it. Only Miss Nielson. Don't feel bad about your exclusion, though. It won't work. You won't be able to prove anything, and I doubt if anyone will ever take two nonentities like yourself seriously."

His eyes came unfocused, then looked past me. I could smell perfume in the stale air of the study. It was Janet's scent. I turned my head and looked at her. She had a gun in her hand, a good, old fashioned .45 automatic looking ridiculously large in her slim grip.

"You killed Ezekial," she accused, her voice harsh and deadly.

"Yes, my dear," Buckley answered. "I've already explained all that to Mr. Slade, here. I'm sure that he can fill you in on the details later."

Janet's gaze wandered to me. The hate left her eyes and was replaced by uncertainty. Our eyes locked for a moment.

Out of the corner of my eye, I saw Buckley turn his gun on Janet, raising the barrel towards her heart. I dove across the desk at him. I was too slow. I fell belly down across the top of the desk. I could feel the press of my revolver underneath me, unreachable as the publisher's gun swung back towards me.

There was a sound like thunder and the top of Buckley's head disintegrated in a flash of heat and light as the .45 slug tore into his face and blew out the back of his scalp. I rolled over to see Janet standing there with the automatic pointing, the barrel smoking.

"Frank," she begged as she let the gun fall, "are you all right?"

"Yeah," I answered, as I levered my way off the desk top. "Thanks for shooting." She nodded numbly as I went to her and held her in my arms. Even smelling of cordite she was sweet. I held her for a long moment pressing her head against my shoulder, then let her loose and picked the gun up with my handkerchief and set it on the table. I pocketed my own rod and looked at the broken remains of the vial on the desk. I had landed on it in my dive and smashed it. The liquid had already soaked into the blotter. The evidence was gone.

"I'd better call Flannigan," I said with a sigh, then reached for Janet again.

Chapter 9

Buckley's death was ruled justifiable homicide. Not that they had much choice; it was Janet's and my word against Buckley's, and he wasn't talking. As to Handler's murder, the evidence was gone. The cops, even Flannigan, wouldn't even listen to me when I gave them the story. From their point of view there wasn't much reason with Buckley dead and no evidence.

I went back to being a gumshoe for hire. I still had to eat, though Janet paid me a nice fee. I wasn't letting myself have any doubts that Handler had played any part in the whole affair. Not, that is, until I got a letter from the late author's lawyers.

The cover letter explained how Handler had left instructions that I should receive the contents of the manila envelope that came with the letter in the eventuality of both his and Buckley's death.

The envelope sat on my desk for a long time while I stared at it. I brought out the bourbon and poured a tumbler full of the amber liquid, but in the end I decided that I didn't need any dutch courage to open it up. I wasn't surprised when three sheets of typing paper fell out. I was when a check joined them. It was made out for ten grand and carried Handler's signature. It was dated the day of his death. For that much money I owed it to him to read what he had written.

> Dear Mr. Slade,
> I feel that it is necessary to give you my thanks, my apologies, and what must pass for an explanation. The latter must be brief, and they will leave you with doubts and questions, but under the circumstances there can be no help for that.
>
> As you read this, you must know that I am now dead and that Ronald Buckley was my murderer. You have also acted as an agent of justice in achieving final vengeance on my late publisher. For that I thank you. You may also realize that you have not been a free agent in this matter. I apologize for that, but there was in fact no other way that I could be sure of the final results.
>
> For some years I have dabbled in what may be called the arcane arts. How I acquired this interest and how I advanced my knowledge aren't relevant now, but after a time I became convinced that such arts do exist and I became proficient in their application.
>
> It was in this manner that I became aware of the fact that Buckley intended to kill me, and

furthermore, that the police would be unable to bring him to justice. Despite my skill, I seemed unable to prevent this turn of events.

That is where you, Miss Nielson, and several others come in. I could not avoid my own death. For reasons that are hard to explain to one unfamiliar with the art, I had no power to affect Buckley's actions. I could, however, under these same restrictions, create agents to avenge me. You are one of these creations. So are the others.

I was aware of a spell, if one wants to think in those terms that allowed the creation of simulacrums and their animation. The process is similar to that used by Rabbi Loew to create the Prague golem, though it is by no means identical. It is important in the ritual to describe the creature exactly and in great detail. That is one facet of my writing where I have always excelled. My books have always been 'realistic', though some of my critics have said that that was a fault. I decided, in any case, to attempt to get my revenge on Buckley in this manner.

My first attempt was Armand, the news stand operator. Not a major character, to be sure, but good enough for the first try. I was successful. The rest, including yourself, came after, each added as my plot elaborated itself.

I was happy with the results, but aware, too, that my time was growing short. Not only was it necessary to create you and your respective pasts as well, but I also had to manipulate you so that my plot would reach completion. I achieved this control by writing down what I wished you to do. You have seen some of these writings. I left them so that you would find them at the appropriate times to guide your actions.

Now, the results have been achieved. You may think this all overly elaborate, but I hope that you can see how this might appeal to an author caught up in the strands of fate. I regard it as my greatest work, my best plot. To an author, working with the very substance of reality rather than mere words on a typewriter is heady stuff. I only hope that wherever my soul goes after my death, that I will be able to see the results of my handiwork.

It may seem to you the greatest vanity to create life to serve my own ends. Perhaps it is. I will have to face judgment on that. As to your own fate, and that of the others, I am uncertain. I do not know whether once created you will vanish again, or instead, live out normal lives. I hope that the latter is the case, for you have served me well and are in a manner of speaking, my children. I must ask you to forgive me for any flaws in your character as I created them, and to forgive me for playing with your life. I hope that the accompanying check will in some way repay these trespasses. I have rewarded the others in a similar manner, especially dear Janet.

Again, you have my thanks and apologies. Whether this explanation serves or not will be for you to decide.

It was signed with a scrawl that might or might not have been Handler's signature. It matched the one on the check.

The doubts that I had been holding at bay all came rushing back chased down by the sour mash in the bottle on the desk. It was crazy, insane, but however weird, it fit the facts. I tried to convince myself that Buckley had written it, or rather some part of him wracked by guilt and seeking punishment. That was the rational theory.

I had to find out or I would be the one hunted into madness. I called the lawyers. They were cordial, but not of much help. They had received the envelope the day of Handler's death and had forwarded it after the inquest into Buckley's death. They had seen no reason not to comply with the instructions, but they could not prove whether they had come from Handler.

The only help the bank gave me was in accepting the

check. I walked out ten thousand richer, but no wiser as to whether it was genuine or a forgery. I still don't know.

In the end, I got nowhere trying to prove things one way or the other. I spent a week drinking and wondering if I was going to disappear off the face of the earth. When that got too much for me I wondered if I would know whether I had disappeared.

It was Janet who brought me out of it. She was good therapy, and after a while, I wasn't even afraid of the dark, not as long as she was near me.

When they read Handler's will, it turned out that he had left Janet the rights to his last book. They brought in a cool million at the auction not including the movies. Despite the fact that she was rich, Janet decided she wanted to marry me. It was a grand affair. Flannigan was the best man and Josephine LaTouche sang "Oh Promise Me." After the wedding I gave up being a P.I. I moped around for a bit until Janet decided that I should put my hand to writing. My publisher says that there's a touch of Handler in my work. I don't know, I never read the stuff.

I never have told Janet about that last letter from Handler. It has always seemed best to spare her the doubts. I've never been able to make up my mind, and now I don't really care if I was born of flesh and blood or if I was hatched on a typewriter. But I'm still not sure.

About The Author

Greg Fowlkes is a writer and musician. His day job for the last three decades has been as a programmer in the telecommunication industry. He obtained a Master's degree in Physics from the University of Wisconsin. Currently he lives outside of Madison with his long time companion Irene and two Shiba Inu dogs named respectively after a samurai actor and one of that actor's more famous roles. When not walking dogs, he enjoys reading, making craftsman furniture and playing the guitar and mandolin. His latest musical project is learning the playing style of gypsy jazz guitarist Django Reinhardt.

About The Publisher

Intrepid Ink, LLC provides full publishing services to authors of fiction and non-fiction books, eBooks and websites. From editing to formatting, from publishing to marketing, Intrepid Ink gets your creative works into the hands of the people who want to read them.

Find out more at www.IntrepidInk.com.

Coming Soon from The Fictional Press

Wizard at Law
Egil Njalsson is an attorney at law and a license wizard. This collection of novellas documents his cases, which all have a supernatural element and more than a touch of danger.

Tequila Visions
Thorwald Ostergard was a typical graduate student working on his Ph.D. thesis until one night he took a drink from a strange bottle of tequila. When he woke up he found himself in an enchanted world populated by trolls, witches and dwarves, and those were just the good guys. Drafted to go on a quest across this mysterious island he must face danger at every turn to save the world from the Castelan and his Black Riders. But his biggest challenge is to find his love and himself.

Cargo from Paradise
Erwald Thorsen was captain of the tramp space freighter the DuNix. He and his Estroli partner Fang that Gleams would take just about anything from one planet to the next. That's how they found themselves carrying a cargo of agricultural machinery from Paradise to Marshall along with a beautiful passenger. Of course the cargo turned out

not to be farm equipment, and the two find themselves chased across the galaxy by smugglers only to find themselves caught in the middle of a planetary rebellion.

Ice Viking
Authun was captain of the ice ship Snow Bear. He was a Viking and good at it. But then he finds himself stranded on the ice and his ship stolen. To get it back he must confront Eorl Moerck in his impregnable fortress Grey Rock, rescue his crew, and chase the thief across the vast expanses of ice.

Blood Red Sands of Mars
Erik McKernan was the chief constable. On Mars. He had a murder to solve, politics to deal with and a beautiful reporter from Earth to complicate matters. All while trying to survive a hostile environment and whoever was trying to kill him.

Made in the USA
Monee, IL
27 August 2021